Books by Bert Bartz

IdioTsynchrasies

When the Lollies Bloom: Sweet with Some Bitter, Bitter with Some Sweet

The Fail Mary Plan as Told to Mrs. Mangin: The
Chuckables of On-line Dating

Conquering the Crow: Coincidences

You Are Now Entering: Challenges

The Man I Almost Met for 18 Minutes in an Edinburgh Coffee Shop

The Man I Almost Met
for 18 Minutes in an
Edinburgh Coffee Shop

Bert Bartz

ARCHWAY
PUBLISHING

Archway Publishing books may be ordered through booksellers or by contacting:

Archway Publishing
1663 Liberty Drive
Bloomington, IN 47403
www.archwaypublishing.com
1 (888) 242-5904

ISBN: 978-1-4808-6405-4 (sc)
ISBN: 978-1-4808-6406-1 (e)

Library of Congress Control Number: 2018947877

Print information available on the last page.

Archway Publishing rev. date: 06/12/2018

Dedicated
To Ken and Seth.
This is my final time warning you guys:
don't ever go on a cruise!

Special Thanks
To Gale,
for your inspiration for Officer Tipsy
and your friendship.

Introduction

The Price of Coffee

Newsflash to myself. I spend more on coffee than on cable TV.

ON SHORE:
Two Important Things Happened

The first was Bimsa, that dumbass friend of mine, convinced me the only way to travel was by cruise ship. After listening to him, I wanted to kill myself, but only after I killed him first.

The second was an Edinburgh coffee shop, where I almost met a man for 18 minutes.

ON SHORE:
The Famous 18 Minutes

Eleven months ago, prior to when there was a Bimsa and me, I made a visit to Edinburgh. This was in the late-summer-heading-into-autumn time of year. The purpose of my visit to Edinburgh was none; it was merely an item of curiosity as I had never been there.

Further to that point, I had a second item on my Scotland agenda, which was to visit the Shetlands. Why? Because I had never been there. I did get admonished by a Scottish taxi driver for my intended visit to the Shetlands. The Shetlands are above the Scottish mainland, in the roaring, cold North Sea almost directly between Norway and Iceland. I almost admonished myself for this adventure, given that I had flown in days before from the lower latitudes close to the equator. Now I was wearing anything heavy and woolen. I slept in my Minnesota socks.

Back to the admonishment. This admonishment occurred, mind you, as the opinionated Scottish (is this redundant?) taxi driver drove me from my Edinburgh hotel to the airport. I was scheduled to try my first run with FlyBe airlines to Sumburgh Airport, the biggest airport in the Shetlands. The biggest airport in the Shetlands that nicely accommodates any jet in the range of twenty-four passengers. Sumburgh also has a luggage conveyor belt that can easily handle up to five suitcases at a time. Surely I jest.

Not.

The taxi driver asked me why I was going to the Shetlands. He pointed out that it was cold and dark. I explained I had never been there and I was, as a result, curious as to why people live in a cold, dark, and treeless land. There are no trees in the Shetlands. It has been explained to me that the winds coming over the islands is so fierce that trees cannot stand for very long. However, given the history of the Shetlands, I'm likely to believe the Vikings landed one afternoon and decided, after a frenzy of pillaging and quaffing liters of mead, to chop them all down. And then, with the usual Viking sense of humor, they added some fun to the whole event by distributing a zillion sheep.

Either way, the taxi driver delivered quite a lecture on the subject.

SCOTTISH TAXI DRIVER: I've lived in Edinburgh for over twenty-five years and I never once have been to the Shetlands.

ME: Never? Well, that seems odd, given that the Shetlands are known for so many things.

DRIVER: If you mean sheep. There are more sheep than people. No wonder. Nothing to do up there. And cold as a snowman's tit.

ME: From what I've been reading, there are many items of interest. Birds, for example.

DRIVER: Now what do I need with birds? We've got a heapload of birds right here in Edinburgh.

ME: There must be something of interest. It looks so beautiful in pictures.

DRIVER: How much did you pay for your flight?

ME: About two hundred pounds. Not much.

DRIVER: Ah, but you see, lass, for two hundred pounds, I could be sunning myself in the Canary Islands.

ME: Good point.

DRIVER: Hope you have a good time, Mary Doll. We are now at your terminal. FlyBe is just there.

ME: I hope we're not flying a prop.

DRIVER: You'd better hope you're not. The winds are a con-stant bluster up there. Could land you in the ocean.

Now why do I talk to cab drivers? How was that ending remark going to bolster my confidence?

Before I had decided to undertake that journey, I had never even heard of FlyBe airlines. There are so many jokes I could make about the name alone.

Just before heading back to my hotel to meet up with the confidence-boosting taxi driver, I decided to walk up the hill to the nearest coffee shop. The short journey took me toward the main castle, the front of which was guarded by a bronze replica of a Scottish soldier in full military garb, including a bushy mustache, boots, a gun, and a tall, black, winged monkeys hat. He was seated astride a massive, muscled stallion. The soldier peered at me. I swear his cold, metal lips were formulating a question. "Why are you going to the Shetlands?"

Thank God my coffee was finally in front of me. I popped in and headed straight for the counter to order my double-tall chestnut praline. And to pick up my requisite souvenir coffee mugs to carry back home.

While the barista was making my morning elixir, I noticed a couple of gentlemen sitting by the window. They were occupying a combo couch and dual overstuffed chairs setup. One man, on the couch, was facing the other man, on one of the overstuffed chairs. I noticed they were engaged in a nonstop and highly animated dis-cussion. I tried to imagine why two men would be in a discussion of that nature because, from my perspective, men don't usually en-gage in discussions about their feelings. And their discussion was definitely on some emotional plane. *Maybe they were gay and having a lovers' quarrel?*

No. I finally overheard some tidbit about the man on the over-stuffed chairs regarding his wife or girlfriend or something.

I made a beeline. I wanted to sit on that couch by those windows.

And there was room. So I used my best I-don't-know-any-better American manners and asked if they wouldn't mind if I shared the couch or the other chair. The man sitting on the couch replied that there was no problem whatsoever and invited me to sit down. He was gracious.

And there was something about his face that stuck with me.

COFFEE SHOP MAN: Please. Choose whichever you prefer. You can sit either on the couch or the chair. Of course, if you sit on the couch, you can stare at this guy (he points to his companion). He's the good-looking one.

ME: Thanks. I'll just plop my coat and grab my coffee. Thank you so much!

MAN: No problem. Happy to accommodate.

I walked back to the counter to fetch both my coffee and my bag with the two souvenir Scotland mugs. Actually, I never use my souvenir coffee mugs at home for coffee. They are used for tea. Today, those Scottish mugs are proudly displayed on my breakfast tray near the refrigerator. They remind me of a mission I had yet to make.

I took my mugs and my hot chestnut praline coffee and chose to sit down on the overstuffed chair. In doing so, however, it was not my intention to stare at the man on the overstuffed chair even though the couch man had explained his friend was the better looking of the two. It was my intention to have a perfect sightline of the man on the couch who, in my opinion, was the more interesting of the two.

That short hour of time, before I met the opinionated Scottish taxi driver, I spent sipping my coffee and reading items on my phone. I had nothing of any sort to read on my phone. I had long since checked the morning news from the US, which was nothing more than indigestion provoking. I had already checked in for my flight. I had already ordered my taxi. I hadn't packed because my run up to the Shetlands would only be overnight to test out if I liked them or not.

The short hour, therefore, was not really to drink my coffee but to see if the man on the couch would start a conversation with me. He knew I was American. (Sometimes people confuse my accent with Canadian. No probs.) He was in close range. I gave him every reason, from my amicable voice, to believe I was open to a conversation.

The time to run back to the hotel was quickly approaching. I had about 18 short minutes. So I had to lower myself to gutter level. I made an audible comment, something on the order of "Oh no, my flight just got canceled!" I thought it might break the ice.

The man on the couch enquired about that. *Yes, victory!* I explained that my flight back to the US was canceled due to an impending hurricane and I was not sure what I was going to do.

"You're welcome to stay in Edinburgh as long as you wish."

That statement, by the man on the couch, was said with substantial grace, charm, and subtle invitation.

To this, I replied, "I might just do that." I smiled. I smiled so hard my jaw hurt and I was certain my face was now permanently glued in that position.

So there it was—that moment in time when two people talk to each other, say nothing, say everything, yet no communication takes place. That small moment in time when the paths of two people cross. A blip on the radar. Why did it happen? Was this a missed chance? Was it random? Was it coincidence?

So now back in the US, as I had my many mornings of tea—in the mug with the picture of the Scottish piper on the front—I think about those 18 minutes in that coffee shop.

And I realize I need to go back.

CRUISE TIPS:
Always Pick First Prize

If you come across a contest for winning a cruise, run away. Consolation prize is a cruise for two, anywhere in the world. First prize is to stay at home.

ON SHIP:
Officer Tipsy

O fficer Tipsy had her own bright-green motor cart she deftly moved from deck to deck faster than an Olympic sprinter. She was first in line for the morning's breakfast buffet, monopolizing the British bacon section so she could assemble "a proper bacon bap with ketchup and mustard," first in line for afternoon scones and clotted cream, first in line for dinner on Italian night, and most important, first in line to grab a prime viewing spot in the open atrium bar-cum-dance floor.

Officer Tipsy liked her rusty nails and not a night went by without her imbibing in a couple. double Drambuie and double Scotch. She added a small twist of lemon to gussy it up.

Her green scooter was meant to be a replica of a favorite antique golf cart that she used to move around in her neighborhood at home. She had bought the golf cart at an auction. "A steal," she told me.

TIPSY: A British Racing Green, antique, one-of-a-kind Elmco. Found it at a garage sale. Dusted it off, buffed and polished it, and now it's as good as new. I run the entire neighborhood from it.

Officer Tipsy still had bright reddish-gold hair, green eyes, and a beautiful smile. She asked us to guess her age. I thought maybe in her seventies. Hard to tell. She hinted she was in her eighties, but I think that's just to throw us off. Big boobs. Sturdy legs. We could see that if and when she ever gets out of her motor cart, she could do some damage to an unsuspecting young cabin boy.

TIPSY: Nope. Don't like the young ones. They bore the bejesus out of me. I want someone who knows what they're doing down there.

BIMSA: Amen

TIPSY: Give me experience. Rough and ready.

BIMSA: Like Teddy Roosevelt?

TIPSY: I was thinking more of the A-Team. Whoever that guy was with the cigar.

BIMSA: Stay away from the cabin boys then. They all want boys themselves.

TIPSY: Right. I hang more around the upper-class restaurants and bars. Anyway, the rich old gentlemen hang there and are usually good for a round or two.

ME: Of drinks?

TIPSY: What did you think I meant?

CRUISE TIPS:
Embarkation

Before you Embark, there are two important things to do. Number One:

Learn the difference between the terms Embark and Debark. First, this will help you walk onboard the ship when you are meant to do so, rather than walk off the ship when you are not meant to do so. Also, it will prevent you from confusing the Immigration officer. If you write on your Immigration form that you Embarked on Day 14 and Debarked on Day 1, the Immigration Officer will likely throw you in the slammer for being either on drugs or just plain old barking mad.

Number Two:

Having been through previous Embarkation exercises, and knowing they are long in duration, congested, hot, and full of confused people (mostly the crew), I highly suggest that embarkation is only attempted after throwing back several shots of Scotch, popping three muscle relaxers, and smoking a joint the size of a 747. Which, of course, you will wish you were on.

Try to maintain your cool when the $6-an-hour Embarkation agent asks you for your 500 pages of ticketing documents, carefully pages through them for twenty minutes while continually appearing confused, and then finally asks you to fill out a health declaration form. No problem. The last hurdle before you are allowed to cross through those pearly gates that magically transfer you from land to ship.

You ask for a pen. The agent doesn't have a pen. Of course. Why would an agent—whose job is to embark a zillion people, whose job it is to ensure their paperwork is correct, whose job it is to streamline the process—have a pen?

There are five thousand people in the Embarkation terminal and not a single pen to be found. And if you didn't have a health problem previously, your blood pressure has just shot through the roof and your bladder is begging to die.

There is enough luggage floating around to camp out in Tibet for a year. And no Yeti in sight.

ON SHIP:
Bimsa Takes on Officer Tipsy

Officer Tipsy came rolling around in her green motorized cart. It was modeled after her British Racing Green Elmco golf cart she used at home to patrol her neighborhood. In fact, she was given the name Officer Tipsy because she made it her daily mission to take stock of the neighborhood, watch who was coming and going, note any strange goings-on, and report suspicious activities. She was her own self-appointed law enforcement officer.

Officer Tipsy wheeled up to Deck 16 to join in evening martinis and ship gossip, which she referred to as "goss." "What's the goss?" she'd ask at the start of each evening's adult beverage hour.

BIMSA: I have to tell you, OT (Bimsa shortened her name.), you can down more booze in one night than I can in my lifetime.

TIPSY: I like my evening cocktail.

BIMSA: Evening cocktail? You sound like a 1950s Grace Kelly movie. I expect Cary Grant to come jumping out of the woodwork.

TIPSY: If only.

BIMSA: Not my type.

TIPSY: Thank God. You've taken up too many available men as it is.

BIMSA: I doubt you and I have the same taste in men.

TIPSY: Do you like Sean Connery?

BIMSA: Who doesn't?

TIPSY: Then we have a problem.

BIMSA: Do you like George Michael?

TIPSY: Too young.

BIMSA: He can look under my kilt anytime. Anyway, it hardly matters since he's dead, but nevertheless, we have a common understanding of our choices in male material.

TIPSY: I'll stay away from yours if you'll stay away from mine.

BIMSA: Believe me. I have no interest in men in wheelchairs or toting oxygen tanks.

ME: Will you two shut up! You're driving me insane.

BIMSA: What is your problem?

ME: I'm grumpy. I can't eat and I have to limit the booze.

BIMSA: Because?

ME: Because I've picked up too much weight on this stupid cruise. I think my pilot light went out.

TIPSY: What pilot light?

ME: My metabolism pilot light. I think I doused it. With alcohol.

BIMSA: Well then, go get laid. I did.

ME: Crew again?

BIMSA: Not just any crew. The Cruise Director. Mr. Bingo.

ME: Seriously? That guy is as big as an apostrophe and has an annoying voice like Betty Boop on some serious dope.

BIMSA: I'm not interested in his height and he never speaks when we're in the throes of passion.

TIPSY: Oh God. I think I'm about to barf my martini and both olives.

ME: The entire crew is gay. There is no one to get laid with.

TIPSY: King's English.

ME: No one with whom I can get laid. How about that? The same problem no matter how I formulate the sentence. I need to wake up sore.

BIMSA: OMG! Yes. Wake Up Sore—our group motto.

Remember girls, sign the check before you leave, know the person you're leaving with, and Wake Up Sore!

ME: Alice is probably getting more action than I am.

BIMSA: Bite your tongue, woman! That lass is too young to be doing anything of that sort. If I find any young man snooping around her, I shall challenge him to a duel.

TIPSY: With what? Dueling bagpipes?

BIMSA: What about these initials carved on your little green Mercedes here? RSM?

TIPSY: Never you mind you babbling gay Scotsman. That's for me to know and for you to go take your kilt and jump off the deep end.

ME: Whoops. I think you hit a nerve, Bimsa.

BIMSA: Ah. Methinks there's a pretty rude story attached to those initials.

TIPSY: That's it. I'm taking my martini and rolling my magic green boy down to the casino. You two can stay up here and continue to piss people off.

BIMSA: Well, don't get your knickers in a twist.

TIPSY: I'm not about to give the details of my sex life to the likes of you, you perverted bowl of haggis.

ME: Bimsa! Look! Quick!

BIMSA: What? What?

ME: Is that who I think it is?

TIPSY: Ah—now that's an attractive man.

BIMSA: That's not an attractive man. That's the pain-in-the-ass mystery man who keeps popping up out of the blue.

TIPSY: Who is it?

ME: Parv. His name is Parv.

CRUISE TIPS:
Shows from Hell

Don't pay for shows. Ever. The price of hell should already be included in your ticket.

The good news is most of the time you can just wander in and watch a show. This freedom of choice compensates for lack of talent.

If I could give a first prize to the worst act on earth, I would give it to the four gentlemen who attempted to imitate the Beatles. Hell is listening to the "Third Year in a Row National Champions of Winning Worst Impression Ever of the Beatles." The hair was right. The suits were close. But I doubt these guys know the concept of "in tune." Good thing the bar was close.

ON SHIP:

It's All Fun and Games until Someone Gets Hurt

Here are the forms of entertainment routinely offered. Karaoke. East Wisconsin Falls Women's Knitting Club. (The Tatting Club also meets but don't confuse the two because for one thing, the Tatting Club, "tats" and for another, hails from Forest City Iowa.) The Best Bible Quotes Club (like there are any "bad" Bible quotes?). The Sing-Along Club. Don't be fooled. Sing-Along is not the same as karaoke. Sing-Along is equivalent to a geriatric choir. They gather around the piano while a member of the entertainment crew, a twenty-year-old Macedonian named Dimitri who had taken an immediate fancy to Alice at the onset of the cruise, distributes sheet music.

Dimitri dispenses soft serve vanilla chocolate twist cones on Deck 16 when he's not leading the afternoon session of "voices from hell." Bimsa did not catch on to this fact until he eventually noticed Alice joining in for rounds of *Sweet Caroline* and *Karma Chameleon*. "Loving could be easy if the colors were like my dreams. Red, gold, and ..."

A rehearsal embarks with some small amount of instruction from Dimitri. Alice had to Google to figure out what those songs were.

The main event, the mother of all events, the king of events, is the one event for which everyone would line up for hours as though they were attending a once-in-a-lifetime rock concert. Like "Elvis Comes Back to Life and Sings Bieber Favorites." Wait for it. Yes, folks. I'm talking about that age-old game of fun that never ceases to amuse the mindless. Bingo! Who can resist bingo?

Officer Tipsy races her green cart ahead of everyone without displaying a shred of emotion. Using a walker? Forget it. Officer Tipsy will mow you down. In a wheelchair or carrying an oxygen tank? Sorry for you, dude. Officer Tipsy loves bingo and by God, she's going to be first in line to get her cards. She carries her own dauber with the initials RSM, but she won't let on what those initials mean. Bimsa has put Alice on the mission to see if she can extract information from Tipsy.

BIMSA: Take away her wheels. She'll sing.

ALICE: That's so cruel, Uncle Bimsa. She's just a nice old lady who likes to play bingo.

BIMSA: And throw down vats of booze. I'm pretty sure those initials belong to some guy she ditched on another ship.

ALICE: Maybe to her husband?

BIMSA: Husband my ass. Find some old pro golfer who looks worn down from rough sex with Tipsy and that's your guy.

ALICE: Not everyone is like you, Uncle Bimsa.

BIMSA: Thank God! They'd be stealing all the good ones. And stay away from that Dimitri guy!

ALICE: Uncle, he's really super nice. A gentleman.

BIMSA: A gentleman? I bet. I bet he says "thank you" after he's had his hands all over your teenage ass.

ALICE: Uncle Bimsa! Dimitri isn't like that. He's sweet. He would never touch me without my permission.

BIMSA: Just make sure you don't give it to him! Remember, we are about to see your parents and I have no qualms about spilling the beans to my brother. Straight as he is. And what happened to that nice boy Graham somebody-or-other from Glasgow?

ALICE: There's no beans to spill. He's a nice guy. And he's studying to be a veterinarian. And Graham is boring.

BIMSA: Boring? What does that mean? Oh, I know. He doesn't comb his hair with Gorilla Snot and have earbuds plugged into his ass night and day. And why would some ship guy become a veterinarian? There are no animals on ships. As a rule. Except for the loonies who insist on bringing a service animal the size of a gnat. Not sure what "service" that animal is providing. "Here's Sprinkly, my miniature miniature. I need him to fetch my wheelchair."

ALICE: On that subject, don't do yoga on the artificial turf by the top club. I saw dogs peeing on it this morning.

BIMSA: Oh, great Jesus. Is nothing sacred on this ship?

ALICE: Didn't see any poop though! Cruise jobs are just a means to an end for him.

BIMSA: Like they'd be anything else?

ALICE: Seriously, Unc—he wants to open a practice. Large animals. Horses!

BIMSA: Eeeww. That conjures up so many images.

Officer Tipsy comes roaring up in her bright green golf cart look-alike.

TIPSY: I almost ran straight into some massively fat cow. I asked her, "Why don't you get your fat butt out of that chair and do something? Jesus woman, you're half my age." And you know what she told me? "I can't do anything about my weight. I have a thyroid condition." And I said, "Jesus H. Christ, girl. Thyroid condition, like hell! You don't have a thyroid condition. You have a 'sit on my fat ass and eat donuts' condition! Go out and get laid! Go find some super-hot guy and grab his balls until he cries for his mama!"

BIMSA: That's right, Tipsy. What's our motto?

TIPSY and BIMSA: (in unison) Wake Up Sore!!!

CRUISE TIPS:
Mustard

Once you've pushed and shoved and sweated your way through a million passengers, and just as you think you've escaped with your life, and just as you start to settle down in your cracker box of a cabin, you will be forced to report to a central area, pushing and shoving and sweating through the same million passengers.

Then you will be totally humiliated by being forced to place an orange sponge over your head and tie it off at the waist so you look something like a giant bratwurst.

Next, you will be asked to demonstrate you know how to properly dress yourself like a large bratwurst.

And finally, you will fight to keep from falling asleep as you are forced listen to the world's worst infomercial about safety while members of the crew attempt to keep you awake with cattle prods.

Buyer beware: If you miss this event, whether by mistake or on purpose, you will be punished. Captain's choice. You may be placed in the brig or asked to eat at the buffet.

P.S.: The name of this event is "muster." For the longest time, I thought it was "mustard." Who knew?

ON SHIP:

Eating Toast

W̲e quickly established some rituals on board. Office Tipsy was definitely a big part of them. Each morning, she ran her scooter up to Deck 16 to meet me for breakfast. I had found a place, starboard and aft. For those who aren't trained in a double-secret Marine-speak, that means I was on the right side of the ship and at the back.

By my second day onboard, I had discovered a group of tables nestled near the coffee and juice station with a great view of the ocean, yet out of danger from freezing winds or sheets of icy rain. I had gone to that same spot each day, and the crew began to treat it as my spot. They immediately showed up with a glass of cold orange juice on ice and coffee with whole milk and sugar. They left me alone for hours on end if I just wanted to sit in the company of my laptop. On a couple occasions, I left my sweater on the back of a chair, and they simply left it knowing I would eventually come back for it.

Officer Tipsy knew my secret spot. She bullied her way to the front of the buffet each day to grab hot, juicy pieces of British bacon, and I bullied my way to the side where I could find double-crispy American bacon. Tipsy made ketchup and mustard baps on soft rolls. She lorded over the entire bread section until they brought out the assortment of buns and then she dug and scrounged through them until she found one type that was bap-comparable.

I also made a beeline for the bread section, but my ritual was different. The toast was already made each morning. This was great. I didn't have to stand in front of some industrial-size toaster waiting for two slices of bread to tediously move over the hot wires as though they were slowly drifting down a lazy river. God bless the breakfast crew members who had long since made the toast, judging from the color and texture, in an oven. That's a proper piece of toast. I like the toast hard and crunchy from the slower process in an oven. Ideally, the pieces would then be stood up in a good old-fashioned toast holder. But alas, when there are five thousand passengers on a ship, that would be a little difficult to achieve, so toast had been laid in a giant warming pan and you could fish out the pieces you wanted with large tongs.

I took a large dinner plate on which I placed three pieces of toast, three pats of butter, one dollop of raspberry jam, one dollop of strawberry jam, and one dollop of peanut butter. Tipsy watched me as I broke off small pieces at a time, spreading butter and raspberry jam on each little section. That was my starting point.

TIPSY: Now what are you doing?
ME: Ah, here comes the best part—peanut butter and bacon.
TIPSY: Sounds ghastly
ME: You have to try it. Delicious. Toast, peanut butter—a bit of strawberry jam is optional but nice—and finally, a very crispy piece of American bacon.

Officer Tipsy found this combination so delightful, that she eventually abandoned her bap in favor of her newly discovered peanut butter and bacon. I had long since turned Bimsa on to these little delights, so if he got out of bed early enough, he would mosey on up to the secret spot to join us.

TIPSY: Can you guess where my accent is from?
BIMSA: Haven't the slightest.

TIPSY: Blackpool. By way of Halifax.

BIMSA: Blackpool. OK, lady from Blackpool, can you guess where my accent is from?

TIPSY: Well that's not difficult. You're obviously from Scotland.

BIMSA: Well that's bloody no good, is it? Any fuckwit can tell I'm from Scotland, but the question is, where in Scotland?

TIPSY: How the hell should I know that? A Scottish accent is a Scottish accent.

ME: Unless you are in the Shetlands. I have to put on closed captions when I'm talking to anyone in the Shetlands to understand what the hell they are saying.

BIMSA: Do you have any news reports today, Officer Tipsy?

Bimsa called her Officer Tipsy—OT—because she got dirt on the other passengers. She knew who was sneaking around to other cabins and which crew members slept with each other. She knew who was on the ship with their mistress and which wives were travelling with their boy-toys.

ME: And why Halifax?

TIPSY: I lived there for a bit. With my second—no strike that—third husband. He was a bit of a wanker. Finally had to kick him to the curb. Too bad. He was hot as pastrami on rye.

BIMSA: Jesus will you two shut up. Back to my question. Any goss today?

TIPSY: I saw one of the officers come out of a cabin early this morning. I'm sure it was to handle a complaint.

BIMSA: A complaint? You mean like "Gee officer, my husband's dick isn't big enough. Can you help?"

TIPSY: I expect it was something like that. I don't find the officers on this cruise particularly interesting. I do, however, think the maître d' in the French restaurant is definitely a "Spank me and I'm yours." I think he's Turkish.

BIMSA: Turkish. Yum! Probably has a big kabob.

TIPSY: Oh, I hope so. I'd like to do a whirling dervish with him in my cabin some night.

ME: You know guys, cruises are not just about sex.

TIPSY and BIMSA: (in unison) Shut your mouth!

CRUISE TIPS:

The Difference between Fore and Aft

For some reason, passengers are expected to take a maritime test once they are onboard. Why do we need to know the difference between fore and aft? Port and starboard? Who the fuck cares?

If you want to have fun with the crew, use the wrong terms. It drives them crazy. Even better, stop an officer and ask in your worst American accent (though that might be redundant), "Which way is it to the front of the boat?" With this single sentence, you have committed a double mortal sin. I promise you the officer will have a meltdown on the spot.

And if you get stopped by other passengers asking directions, just politely respond, "Does it read 'Julie Cruise Director' on my forehead?" And then tell them to fuck off.

ON SHIP:

People Watching

BIMSA: Look over there. Quick!

ME: What am I looking at?

BIMSA: Shrimp Lady.

ME: Shrimp Lady? Why is she Shrimp Lady?

BIMSA: Because she wheeled up to the fried shrimp station, grabbed the tongs, and put about a thousand on her plate. There aren't any left! Not one bloody shrimp.

ME: Maybe Officer Tipsy will report her.

Alice has joined us at the dinner buffet. It's soup night and thus it's the one night when all things are right with the buffet. The diners gather all the vegetables and meat they desire, and then the cooks create a hot pot pho-type soup from their selections. So, all of us agreed to meet on soup night and the rest of the time everyone was on his or her own.

Alice reported information about her friend Dimitri, that they have exchanged email information for keeping in touch post-cruise. In the meantime, she has discovered a French boy. Another passenger. He's travelling with his family. Dumas. Apparently, they named him after the author, but that was all the information Bimsa and I could get out of her. Teenagers are elusive and secretive. Either that or Bimsa and I just bored the hell out of her so she blew us off as much as possible. Too bad. I thought Dumas was kind of a cool name.

TIPSY: Can I join you for a bowl of soup?

BIMSA: Absolutely. But only if you have news to report.

TIPSY: I do, in fact. But it's rather disgusting. Are you up for it?

BIMSA: I'm up at all times.

ME: I think she's referring to your receptiveness to a story. Not your biological inclinations.

TIPSY: Well after I tell this story, I doubt Bimsa will have any inclinations left. I was up having my afternoon martini when I noticed two people over at that railing on the port side.

ME: Intriguing. Go on.

TIPSY: Do you remember that huge young woman I yelled at because she was too fat to get out of her wheelchair and all she does is eat?

BIMSA: Ya.

TIPSY: Ah, but it turns out she does something other than eat after all. Apparently, she is on board with her—yes, I'm going to say this—boyfriend! And they are sharing a cabin! I got all that from one of the stewards, of course. I may have dropped in a tip or two for the intel. The steward had to make "special arrangements" in the cabin for them.

BIMSA: Eeewwww.

TIPSY: Anyway, they were by the railing and she had her hands completely down his pants doing God knows what.

BIMSA: Oh my God! An in-cruise hand job!

ALICE: Uncle Bimsa, that's disgusting.

BIMSA: Just remember you said that the next time you talk about that Dumas perv.

TIPSY: And then to top things off, he put his hands down her pants.

ME: She's still sitting in the wheelchair this whole time—correct?

TIPSY: Indeed. But it didn't appear he was having any trouble finding what he was looking for.

ALL: Eeeewwww.

TIPSY: And this went on for quite some time. I would say two passionfruit martinis and one rusty nail.

BIMSA: I'm not sure I can finish my soup.

ME: I'm not sure I can swallow. Never mind. Erase that.

BIMSA: Oh, but it's such a perfect line.

ME: I think after dinner, I'm going to head straight to the bar.

ALICE: I'm going to find Dumas. I think he's in the casino.

BIMSA: You're too young to be in the casino. How old is this Dumas shady character?

ALICE: He's eighteen.

BIMSA: Or so he says.

ALICE: Unc, he's fine. Don't worry.

BIMSA: I am worried and I have two words for you. Con Doms.

ALICE: I just met him. I doubt we will need that.

BIMSA: No. The right answer would be, "Gee, Uncle Bimsa, there is no need to worry because I am not sexually active."

ALICE: Correct. No need to worry.

BIMSA: ... because ...

ALICE: Bye. Gotta go. Love you!

CRUSE TIPS:
Buffets Are Disgusting

Number One:

People sneeze and cough on the buffet. And each serving instrument is handled about five thousand times. People swirl their fingers around in stuff and place their noses close to sniff and hack phlegm over everything.

What is it with buffets? It must be something to do with the perception there's free food and a lot of it that creates some odd feeding frenzy. The food is not gourmet quality. It's acceptable. But people would attack the platters and bowls and pots as though they had been created by some five-star restaurant.

I watched a woman from Germany fight over a chunk of cheese one time. I watched two women from China fight over their position in the buffet line as everyone gathered waiting for the doors to open. This was especially amusing since they were fighting over position one and position two. I could never figure out what difference it made.

Number Two:

Things not to eat: sour cream, pickles, cheese if already cut, cold meat, boiled eggs, fresh fruit, salad fixings of any type, pâté. Stick to anything cooked on the spot or difficult for body fluids to reach. When in doubt, drink a lot of alcohol afterwards.

ON SHIP:

Bimsa Takes on Parv

Officer Tipsy decided to stick around and watch the excitement. It was evident she couldn't take her eyes off Parv. But I couldn't tell if she was more interested in him or if she just liked a good old row every now and then to keep the excitement going.

Parv had been waving from across the deck, in an attempt to catch our attention and then walked toward us in a fast stride.

Bimsa took a deep breath. Parv wasn't Bimsa's favorite.

PARV: Good evening. I've been trying to catch your attention for several minutes. I didn't want to just walk over here and foist myself on your group.

(He shakes hands with Bimsa and leans forward to place a kiss on my cheek.)

PARV: Hello. May I introduce myself? I'm Parv. And whom do I have the pleasure of meeting?

BIMSA: (whispering to me) OMG. He sounds like that oily character Zoltan Karpathy from *My Fair Lady*.

TIPSY: Good evening. I'm Tipsy.

PARV: I think not. You seem perfectly sober to me.

BIMSA: (whispering to me) Wow. Get a new line, dude.

TIPSY: (giggling) You are so right. At least I wasn't tipsy until I saw you from across the room and all I could think was how this devilishly handsome man was waving at us. That, of course, caused a little stir.

PARV: I thank you for the compliment, although there are far more handsome men on this ship than I.

TIPSY: I highly doubt that. I've seen the captain. He's got a stomach the size of an old wood-burning, pot belly stove. And he really should do something about his teeth. They look like yellowed broken china.

BIMSA: Of course, the captain is your friend, is he not?

TIPSY: Oh dear. I've put my foot in it.

BIMSA: Shit. Specifically, dog shit.

PARV: Not at all. The captain is an acquaintance of mine. Not so much of a friend.

BIMSA: Tell me, brother. Why are you here? What was the big mystery? I thought you were going to get us a free cruise or something. And I dragged my friend and my niece on this floating petri dish upon your suggestion.

PARV: (chuckling) You are indeed correct. I did suggest this would be the cruise to take rather than flying over to the UK. And aren't you having a grand time?

BIMSA: If you call having a grand time slipping and sliding all over and having to take a poop in the world's tiniest bathroom. Sure. I'm having a great time. A super time.

ME: Well, I'm certainly curious. Why did you suggest this cruise to Bimsa? I also thought we were going to have some sort of perk and I haven't seen hide nor hair of anything remotely resembling a freebie.

PARV: Of course. Let me explain. I am here on business with some of my partners. And I have arranged for all of you to be changed to top-deck suites. And yes, I have, in fact, arranged for your cruise and all amenities to be complimentary. Sorry, madam. (He addresses OT.) Not you, of course, as I didn't realize you would be travelling with this party.

TIPSY: Oh no. I'm not travelling with them. I've only just met them in the last few days. Over afternoon tea and scones about which we've now made a ritual everyday around 3:00pm on Deck 16. I will take the liberty of reserving an extra seat. I do hope you will join us.

PARV: I would be delighted.

BIMSA: So, let me get this straight. We're going to change cabins? And haul our suitcases up to the top deck? And how is this being done exactly? And when?

PARV: I've arranged it all. The stateroom attendants will pack everything in your room and unpack it in your new room. You can stop at the front desk and they will give you your new keys.

ME: I don't quite understand why you would do this for us. And why our accommodations are being comped?

BIMSA: Ya. Why the fucking mystery?

TIPSY: I should think you guys would be jumping up and down for joy. I would be if I could get out of this bloody cart.

PARV: I can tell you all over dinner tonight if you will agree to be my guests? You too, Ms. Tipsy, I hope.

TIPSY: I wouldn't miss it for the world.

PARV: Excellent. How would eight o'clock suit everyone? In the Pasta Fagioli on Deck 7? I hope you all like Italian.

BIMSA: I like Italian men.

TIPSY: I like Italian wine. Red

PARV: I shall order a special bottle just for you. And how about you? You are being very quiet.

ME: Well, it's a bit ridiculous in a way. Who meets up with a mysterious man on a luxury ocean liner and then is told he will move all my friends and me to suites, which is probably no less than twenty Gs, and is told that everything from now on will be complimentary? It's—well—weird. And sorry, but I'm a bit skeptical as to what strings are attached? I hate strings.

PARV: No strings, I promise. If you will just agree to meet for dinner, then I shall provide a very logical explanation, I assure you.

BIMSA: You'd better. And there better be aglio olio

TIPSY: And arugula with parmesan

PARV: (laughing) I'm certain all that can be arranged. And you? Do you have a demand for dinner?

ME: Zabaglione. And fresh berries.

PARV: Consider it done. Looking forward to seeing all of you in a few hours.

ME: Don't forget a place for Alice.

PARV: Alice?

BIMSA: Alice is my niece. She's seventeen. Innocent as a spring lamb. So, you'd better not hit on her or your balls will be wrapped around the steering wheel. The fat captain's too.

TIPSY: Oh my. Bimsa is certainly colorful.

ME: He's Scottish. What can I say? I think he just likes to use the word *balls*.

PARV: I assure you I will not be hitting on her. I am far older than seventeen and my tastes have progressed.

TIPSY: Hopefully for eighty-year-olds.

PARV: Madam, you are a delight.

BIMSA: (whispering) I bet she would suck his balls right down the back of her throat. Unless you've done that already?

ME: (whispering) I haven't. But I might think about it.

CRUSE TIPS:

Never Share a Cabin

Number One:
Cabins are rooms from hell.

Number Two:

Cabins are not big enough to swing a cat in. Do you actually know how big a cabin is? A cabin can barely hold two small beds, let alone a bathroom. There *is* a bathroom, which is smaller than those in an airplane. And the bathroom requires you to take a step up. This may sound innocuous, but a great deal of alcohol is consumed onboard ships. So, try stepping up or down anywhere for any reason and you take your life in your hands.

The toilet is set up high from the floor so the human body is not in the correct position to take care of the task at hand. The human body should be somewhat crouched for the bowel system to work. But the cabin toilets are so high that the human is almost forced to stand when attempting to purge the system. Also, the toilet seat is quite cold and one could end up with frostbite on the butt.

ON SHIP:
We Break the News to Alice

W e brought Alice down to the front desk before telling her exactly what had happened. "It's a surprise and you'll love it!" is all we said.

When we got done farting around with the $6-an-hour dumbass behind the counter, and once they'd finally sorted out the keys, we told Alice all about Parv and the mystery move and the upcoming dinner that evening.

ALICE: OMG. I can't believe it!

BIMSA: Neither can we. That sleazy guy is up to something.

ALICE: Who cares? A suite! That's awesome!

BIMSA: Why does every teenager use that word fifty times a day?

ALICE: Why does every old person complain fifty times a day about teenagers using the word *awesome*?

ME: Shut up. Let's just enjoy the moment. Keys in hand. And hopefully I'm not in some dream and I'm about to wake up and find out I'm living in Omaha.

BIMSA: Do people actually live in Omaha?

ME: I'm not sure, but I think it must be something like living in Mongolia. Not quite as good, I suspect.

BIMSA: Here's the deal, Mary-doll. I want to make sure you

escort Alice to her suite and make certain some wanker isn't up there trying to hide in the closet or something.

ALICE: Uncle B, I really don't need someone to escort me anywhere. I'm in college. I get to university and back each day without anyone escorting me.

BIMSA: College is not like some big fancy cruise ship. There are a lot of shady characters walking about. I know—I've been with most of them.

ME: I'm happy to escort Alice. Anyway, her suite is right down the hall from mine, so I want to compare.

BIMSA: This guy Parv is beginning to piss me off. I wonder if he's a gangster?

ALICE: Or maybe he owns a diamond mine in South Africa.

BIMSA: See? That would make sense. He forces people to dig and sweat all day and then walks around here like Mr. Fancy Pants. In fact, I think he's a bit of a Nancy.

ME: "A Nancy?"

BIMSA: You know—soft.

ME: Bimsa, did you look as his tats?

BIMSA: What tats?

ME: Ah, you've never seen him in short sleeves. Giant muscles. Big, stylish beautiful tats.

BIMSA: Stop. You've giving me a stiffy.

ALICE: Uncle!

BIMSA: Tats make me sweat.

ME: Me too.

ALICE: You too are exactly alike. I can't tell where one stops and the other begins.

BIMSA: Stop at the penis.

ALICE: Jesus! You're incorrigible!

BIMSA: And where did you see his tats anyway?

ME: The time I met up with him in Trieste. He took off a jacket and had a soft, forest green polo shirt. Big muscly arms with tats.

Soft light hair on the forearms. Large strong hands. Nails, clean but not too clean.

ALICE: Why is that important?

ME: Because I like a masculine man. If his nails are too clean, then I would think he doesn't do any type of manual labor. Just sits around in an office all day or is driven around by a chauffeur. What good is that? I don't want anyone like me. I want someone the opposite of me. A man.

BIMSA: You might try the other side. You might like it.

ME: I try the other side every night. It's called masturbation.

ALICE: OMG! I can't believe you two.

ME: Listen, Alice. There's a lot to be said about masturbation. You can entirely call the shots. When to start. When to stop. What to touch. How to touch. And if you fall asleep in the middle of it, no one cares.

BIMSA: Who falls asleep in the middle of pulling one off?

ME: Oh, I do all the time.

BIMSA: Well that's the ultimate insult. You bore yourself.

ME: It's not a pretty picture. That's for sure.

The three of us hopped an elevator to the top deck after leaving the front desk with our new keys. We were all on the same deck, the same side, and just a few doors down from one another.

I opened the door to my suite and stood frozen as if I'd been hit with a blast of a Minnesota snow storm in January. Entryway. To the right of me, there was a living room. To the left, a doorway going into a master bedroom. A wet bar. And best of all, a bathroom with a hot tub! Who the hell has a hot tub on a ship?? The balcony stretched out for miles, with the bridge right above us. Bimsa reckoned that was on purpose so the captain could peep down on us with his official maritime binoculars. I didn't care. It was so much better than the cracker box I had just hours earlier.

ALICE: He was right. All your things have been brought up here. Look how your suitcases are laid out with such precision.

ME: Suitcases hell. I'm looking at all the amenities. There's champagne and chocolates on the wet bar. And a cracker basket.

ALICE: And a fridge full of cheese and fruit.

ME: Why would I go anywhere on this tub of a boat? I'll just hang in my hot tub with a glass of bubbly.

We checked out Alice's suite next. It was elaborate but a tad smaller. Still replete with all the amenities and also large enough to drive a Mack truck in. Bimsa's was the same. A veritable suite feast.

The best part was the private deck. For suite guests, there was an area held only for the citizens of Deck 17. A spectacular swimming pool. A bar with lovely crew members checking on your every alcohol need. A spa. Large reclining chairs with nearby blankets should one catch a chill.

I gave it a spin.

ME: I will have a porn star martini, please.

CREW: Certainly, madam.

ALICE: I'll have one as well.

BIMSA: Forget it. She'll have a Porn Star martini without the Porn.

CREW: Perhaps a lighter version? Maybe just the passion fruit juice?

ALICE: Uncle, get a clue. I drink.

BIMSA: Never heard it. Not hearing it. *La la la la la la la la la la.*

ME: (whispering to Alice) I'll give you hits of mine.

ALICE: Cool.

BIMSA: I heard that.

ME: Oh please go fuck yourself.

BIMSA: Oh, how I've tried.

CRUISE TIPS:
Rethink That Idea

Number One:
People who think cruising is fun are out of their minds.

Number Two:
People who think cruising is fun are out of their fucking minds.

ON SHIP:

Tipsy's Past

BIMSA: Do you have children?

The questions kept coming from him as though he were conducting an interrogation in an East German prison. It made me think of that old Cheech and Chong routine: "Sign ze papers old man." Bimsa was going hard. Tipsy ignored him.

TIPSY: No children.

BIMSA: Why not?

TIPSY: Why don't you run a four-by-four head through your rectum and tell me how it feels.

BIMSA: Sweet Jesus, girl—don't make me excited!

TIPSY: Good Lord. I should have known that was the wrong thing to say to him.

ME: You should have said eggplant.

BIMSA: And why are you so gloomy, lass?

ME: Because I wanted exercise. Instead I had a crap yoga class. And where the hell were you, Bimsa, buddy? You were supposed to go with me!

BIMSA: I couldn't. Tipsy and I had an appointment at the salon.

TIPSY: Where he started interrogating me. And he hasn't stopped.

BIMSA: I'm simply trying to find out about the men in your life.

TIPSY: What happened in yoga? How could yoga on a ship be bad? I should think it would be soothing.

ME: It was hell. The not-so-hell part was the constant attempt to hold a position while the ship was rocking back and forth. It's like trying to do yoga on a waterbed.

BIMSA: Now that's a thought!

ME: And then I got the plank Nazi instructor. We did no fewer than thirty planks in an hour. Every inch of my body hurts.

BIMSA: Why don't you run out and find the little Parv guy to rub your hurting parts for you?

TIPSY: Yes—where is Mr. Fantasy Island anyway?

ME: I don't know. I don't think I care.

BIMSA: Bite your tongue! I've seen those tattoos.

ME: I'm suffering from a giant bout of "burning indifference."

TIPSY: Ha! Ask me about it. I've had four husbands and I don't give a second thought to a one of them—fabulous as they were.

BIMSA: (leaning on his elbows and looking starry-eyed) I'm dreaming about them now. I can only imagine.

TIPSY: That's all you could do, my dear Bimsa. Every one of those scallywags was a total he-man. They would chew you up and spit you out.

BIMSA: Stop! I'm drooling. I'm hearing the he-man song in my head.

TIPSY: I would like to kick every last one of them in the goolies. The last bugger left me high and dry in Halifax.

BIMSA: Halifax. Lord almighty. What's there? Snow?

TIPSY: And fish. And water. And cold. The only thing that saved me in Halifax was the Maud Lewis museum.

BIMSA: Who?

ME: Famous artist. Folk art. Also died after having spent a lifetime with some worthless shit.

TIPSY: Amen. Although one of my husbands did have some lovely tattoos on his upper arms.

BIMSA: I'm crying with envy now.

TIPSY: He was a singer.

BIMSA: (mimics fainting)

TIPSY: He was a mariachi. Wore the large sombrero and boots with spurs ...

BIMSA: ... and those tight pants with metal horses running down his outer thighs?

TIPSY: If he were here I would gladly hand him over to you.

BIMSA: He sounds dreamy.

TIPSY: He was dreamy per se. Big dark pool eyes. Thick head of shiny black hair. Large lips. Just the right amount of body hair. Enough so you knew you were with a man. Not so much that you thought you were sleeping with Sasquatch. Spectacular in bed. Voice like Ricky Martin's might be if he had a set of balls.

BIMSA: My nose is running now.

TIPSY: But dumb as fucking rocks. I paid him off. Take your big guitar and *vete* and don't let the hatch of your minivan hit you in the ass.

ME: Tipsy, what about the guy you went cross country with on a Harley?

TIPSY: In India.

BIMSA: Oh my God! Was he Indian? Please, please, please tell me he was!

TIPSY: He was indeed. Looked like Tyrone Power in *The Rains of Ranchipur.*

ME: Technically, that movie was *And the Rains Came*, which was remade into *The Rains of Ranchipur* with Richard Burton.

TIPSY: Tyrone Power bordering on Naveen Andrews.

ME: Holy crap! After he let his hair down in *The English Patient*?

BIMSA: Skip that. Did he let his pants down?

TIPSY: Yes, which was highly unfortunate because he didn't have enough down there to put on a small wienie roasting stick. I would do better with my favorite sexual partner, me. But I do so love India. Fantastic place. Especially the Punjab.

ME: The Punjab. On a Harley. Wow.

TIPSY: It's the memories we create from the chances we take. If we don't put a foot out there, we end up like Eleanor Rigby. And God knows the last person I want standing over me at my funeral is some weird pedophile priest.

CRUISE TIPS:

Shake Hands with No One and Dress in Scrubs

A cruise ship is a floating petri dish. As evidence, notice the antibacterial dispensers at the entrance of every restaurant. Notice the guards stationed next to the antibacterial dispensers who are there to "encourage" you to disinfect your hands. You can, of course, enter said restaurant without immersing your hands in the now almost-useless (because the strength of germs has over-taken the germ-fighting components) antibacterial slime.

But if you do enter without sliming or washing should there be conveniently placed sinks, notice that eyes of contempt are following you across the room and all the way to your table. They will monitor your every move like agents from the Secret Service.

Why, you ask, are there sanitizing conveniences placed at the entrance of every restaurant? Ah! For those new to cruising, they may be unaware of the little-known diarrhea nuclear bomb fuse called Norovirus. The cruise ship virus. The virus that invades your bowels with a vengeance.

Example. A certain someone had just landed at London Heathrow Airport. During the taxi ride into Central London, the super-blabby black cab driver made a specific point to tell the passenger all about how Norovirus had covered the city of London with a special vengeance. The passenger took note but then threw the thought out of mind and checked into a fabulous Park Street suite.

By the time the passenger, several hours later, had joined a friend for dinner at a nearby high-end French restaurant, he could only just stare at his bowl of steaming, cheesy onion soup with beads of sweat appearing under his top lip. The friend signaled the waiter for a glass of Coke. The waiter obliged. The passenger took a sip. The cooling bubbles ran down the passenger's throat. The passenger then ran down the ridiculously narrow, winding staircase to the child's-closet-size bathroom, praying all the way the toilet would be vacant, which it was, thank heaven, and then barely locked the door when the heaving commenced and continued for fifteen straight minutes.

Upon completing round one, the passenger slowly and carefully walked back upstairs only to be attacked by round two, which forced him to run outside and heave on a nearby cluster of bushes and possibly two frightened nearby tourists trying desperately to run out of the way.

This uncontrollable heaving, coupled with nuclear diarrhea, continued without mercy for the next twenty-four hours. Apparently, the Coke didn't help.

Welcome to Norovirus. Especially prevalent on cruise ships. Which was, rumor has it, the birthplace of this human hell.

ON SHIP:
Dinner with Parv

A t exactly eight o'clock that night, Bimsa, Ms. Tipsy, Alice, and I all walked into the Pasta Fagioli on Deck 7. Rolled, in the case of Ms. Tipsy.

TIPSY: I need a horn on this contraption. People just breeze by me as if there were no one else trying to share the deck.

Parv was already in the restaurant and rose to greet us with a large smile and a small wave. He was dressed in one of his famous Polo shirts, in dark merlot, complemented with a semi-shiny, charcoal-grey Dolce & Gabbana jacket.

Ms. Tipsy wore a long sparkly, bright, North Pole-seasonal green evening gown that got a bit lost in her British Racing Green motor cart. She had a long silver necklace draped multiple times around her neck. Matching earrings dangled from above. The only thing she was missing was a tiara. Or an elf riding alongside her.

Alice had on a tasteful, youthful, short, winter-white wool dress with a large black belt buckled around her small waist. Her hair was pulled up in an "everybody's wearing it suddenly" bun on top of her head, but with her small face and butterscotch-blond hair, it was the perfect complement to subtle, but vogue, fashion choices.

Bimsa, as usual, was dressed to the nines. A bit over the top, but that was to draw attention. If he could've, he would have worn a flashy shirt reading "I'm Gay. Call Me or Lose Out" embroidered on the back.

I was dressed in Target.

Parv escorted us to the table and graciously pulled the chair out for each diner. In the case of Ms. Tipsy, he had the steward remove her chair so she could wheel right up to the table.

Alice was seated next to her and I was seated across from her, next to Parv. I quickly changed seats with Alice so I could be staring directly at Parv. I needed to directly see his facial expressions. I was on a mission to get down to the bottom of this man. Not literally. Well, maybe literally. This placed Bimsa across from Alice and next to Ms. Tipsy.

BIMSA: Don't try any funny stuff. My innocent niece is sitting next to you and I'm watching your every move.

PARV: I assure you I have no intentions toward your niece. Beautiful, though she is. Men much younger ...

BIMSA: (interrupting) Boys.

PARV: Yes, boys much younger will be clamoring for her attentions. Tonight, my eyes will be focused on this lovely gathering of people. (staring directly at me with those words coming out of his mouth).

TIPSY: Alice, my dear, I couldn't help but notice your darling black shoes.

ALICE: Thank you, Ms. Tipsy. I was able to snatch these at DSW. I'm in love with them.

TIPSY: And so you should be. The perfect complement to your dress. Although I am curious about one thing.

ALICE: Sure. What?

TIPSY: It seems most young girls these days are wearing spike heels. You can't walk around, although I don't walk but you know what I mean—metaphorically—without seeing girls in rather tight dresses and extremely high heels. I really don't know how they stay on their feet.

ME: Touché. I watch them walk from the parking lot to the building at my office and they look as though they are in miserable pain.

ALICE: Oh Ms. Tipsy, don't get her started. She will tell you all about how spike heels compress the spine and are tantamount to foot binding.

ME: Well, they are. Painful, spine-compressing, ankle-breaking instruments of torture.

ALICE: (chuckling). I like them. But I'm not about to do anything to injure my ankles. I need to keep my whole body healthy and in prime condition so I can be at my peak for competition. I ride.

TIPSY: (excitedly) Do you? How wonderful! Horses, I assume you mean?

BIMSA: OMG, I hope so.

ALICE: (laughing) I do, Ms. Tipsy. Horses. Jumpers. And I'm hoping to qualify for the Olympics.

PARV: That's wonderful, Alice. Good for you! And a marvelous sport.

TIPSY: I so envy you. I've always wanted to be around horses, but they seem so large and overpowering.

ALICE: You just have to know how to control them. You are the boss. You can't let them think they are in charge. Once you let them know who's in control, they settle down like puppies.

BIMSA: 1200-pound puppies.

ALICE: Oh, Uncle. You're such a fraidy-cat!

BIMSA: Yes. I admit it. And that's how I shall stay. I like anything smaller than me. Well, not anything but ...

ME: Bimsa, stop yourself.

ALICE: Anyway, that's the genesis of my flat shoes. I'm protecting my feet and ankles and legs from any type of injury that would prevent me from competing. Plus, I have to clean the stables, brush down the horses, bust open bales of hay, and throw flakes out to the pasture, mix Omolene for their feed boxes, clean and maintain hooves, wipe down their heads and around their eyes with fly wipe, maintain the tack, and on and on and on. And compete. So, I don't have any time for injuries. Flat shoes are part of the program.

TIPSY: Lord oh my! That's a lot of responsibility for a young woman.

ALICE: It's fine. I love horses. I don't know what I would do without them.

ME: I love to smell them. And to kiss their muzzles. And I actually don't mind the smell of a horse barn.

BIMSA: Good grief. Are we talking about horse turds now? Yum.

PARV: (chuckling) On that note, may I order drinks?

TIPSY: You may.

PARV: And what may I get you, Ms. Tipsy?

TIPSY: I would like a pomegranate martini, if you don't mind.

BIMSA: Are those good?

TIPSY: Of course. They're the best.

BIMSA: Of all martinis in the world? How do you know?

TIPSY: I've hosted a contest—in my mouth.

BIMSA: So have I, girl. Not martinis though.

ME: Bimsa. Behave.

PARV: Of course. And the rest of you? What would you like?

BIMSA: A pomegranate martini as well, please.

ALICE: Apple juice on ice with a slice of lemon.

PARV: And what can I get for you?

ME: No whiskey. No more whiskey. I had rusty nails with Ms. Tipsy the other night and I went down in flames. I had "whiskey-mares" all night long. I dreamt of an old friend in Istanbul who was driving my car and he kept bumping into the sides of things. Scraping the hell out of it. I think I'll imbibe a pomegranate martini as well.

PARV: Splendid.

TIPSY: (whispering) He can leave crackers in my bed anytime.

PARV: OK. The drinks are ordered. And I also ordered a bottle each of red and white. I hope you like my choices.

ALICE: I like red.

BIMSA: You can't drink. You're a child.

ALICE: Uncle, there are many things you don't know about me and I can assure you I'm not a child.

BIMSA: I hope that Dimitri fellow hasn't been sniffing around.

ALICE: Uncle B, Dimitri has long since been kicked to the curb. I have another friend. Remember?

BIMSA: Just make sure he's a millionaire.

TIPSY: Oh for Christ's sake, Bimsa. Get a clue. Girls of seventeen this day and age are not exactly children. Alice seems to have quite a head on her shoulders.

PARV: While we are waiting for our drinks, please avail yourselves of the menu. I can assure you the spaghetti Bolognese, although a common dish, is anything but common as made by this superb chef. The aglio olio is also delicious as well as the spinach fettucine *ai frutti di mare*.

TIPSY: I'm zeroing right in on the beef pappardelle.

PARV: Also delicious, and I assure you all the pasta is cooked to perfection.

The waiter had already placed a basket of bread on the table along with a small container of butter tabs. Bread and butter—my personal crack cocaine. Lifting the white cloth draped across the basket revealed several delicious smelling selections that appeared to have come straight from the oven. I broke the ice by taking a thick slice of French bread and two pieces of cold Irish butter and then passed the basket to Ms. Tipsy. She secured her selections, set them on the small plate to her left, and took a sip of her martini. Eyeing Parv, she set off a new course of conversation.

TIPSY: So, what is it you do?

The whole table stopped cold. We've been asking Parv this question for months, and received nothing but a whopping bucket full of mysterious bullshit answers.

PARV: (smiling faintly) This is my business.

CRUISE TIPS:
Choose Wisely on Sea Days

Find a quiet corner and hide. Far back on the All-You-Can-Eat, Coughing, Farting, Sneezing, Incurable-Pox Buffet Deck is good. After the throngs of fine dining connoisseurs have left.

Hide. If you don't, you will find yourself sitting with the Knifty Knitters Club from Sheboygan Wisconsin. Right wing. Religious. Women should be seen-and-not-heard, child-bearing, cooking, and sewing machines. Apparel from hell. Midwestern accents. Hairdos from Ethel's Beauty and Knitting Supplies Shop. Or is it Ethel's Beauty Supply and Bait Shop? I get so confused.

Good thing there is a bar nearby.

ON SHIP:
Dinner with Parv Part 2

W̲e are all staring.

TIPSY: What the hell do you mean, "this is my business."? Why the obfuscation? Come out with it.

PARV: I assure you, Madam Tipsy. I am not deliberately trying to be mysterious. It was meant to be a surprise but obviously went awry.

BIMSA: To quote Tipsy, "Out with it then."

(Parv casually picks up the bottle of Côte du Rhone and begins topping off the glasses. He then gestures to the waiter to bring another bottle.)

ME: We're waiting.

PARV: (clearing his throat) This is my business. Nothing hidden in the message. This is the business I'm in.

ALICE: Cruise lines?

PARV: (chuckling softly) No. Not exactly. That's somebody else's business.

TIPSY: Then what business, exactly, do you have on this ship?

PARV: I own it.

(Again, the table went silent, all eyes focused on Parv.)

ME: You own this ship?

PARV: I own several ships.

BIMSA: "Several" ships?

PARV: Well, I say "I," but it's really a group of investors. I'm just one of the investors. But this particular ship, of which I'm quite fond, is by its largest percentage mine.

ME: Which is how you got us the suites.

PARV: Yes. The suites are generally held for me and my guests on any sailing.

ME: For which we have to do what?

BIMSA: Ya buddy. For which she has to do what?

PARV: I assure you no one has to do anything. Except enjoy. Which I hope you will do.

TIPSY: Dear sir, I've been around too long and have had too many husbands to imagine there isn't some sort of catch.

PARV: Isn't it possible I simply enjoy your company and wish to have you as my guests? Simple as that?

BIMSA: No.

ME: Hell no. I'm with Tipsy. I don't get it. I don't know what you are expecting.

PARV: Well of course you are welcome to go back to your original cabins. I don't want to make you upset.

BIMSA: I'm not that nervous.

PARV: Then may I ask, what is the cause of your concern?

ME: My concern is I don't understand money. I don't understand what it's like to have the kind of wealth you have. I don't understand people who have that kind of wealth. I don't understand their perspective of the world. Or lack of perspective.

PARV: Just because people have money doesn't mean they lack perspective.

ME: I live paycheck to paycheck. I literally watch my mobile phone in case it lights up with the "you've been paid" message. I wring my hands if that message doesn't come through on time. I have no more than $200 in my checking account at any time.

BIMSA: Which is $200 more than most people have.

ME: I throw stuff in my shopping cart and then start tossing it out when I reach the checkout counter. I shop at Target when I'm feeling a little richer than usual. Otherwise it's Wally World. I eat Cheez Whiz. I fly coach and feel lucky to be in an airplane rather than a Greyhound. My designer clothes are from TJ Maxx. And always one season off. I read People in the store so I don't have to pay for it.

BIMSA: You shop at Tarjhaaay? I can't afford Tarjhaaay!

TIPSY: My dear Parv, I am curious. What would be your motive to take a raggedy band of people such as these and make them your special pets?

PARV: I assure you they are not my pets. But my prizes. Especially this woman. She has intrigued me. She has fascinated me. I have not met anyone like her before.

ME: Jesus you sound like a movie out of the 1950s. Louis Jourdan shit.

PARV: See? This is exactly what I like about you, your honesty.

TIPSY: I can give you honesty. I had four husbands. They all were losers. And they were all the worst in bed. They had no idea what to do "down there."

BIMSA: What they needed was a good man.

TIPSY: I'm beginning to think so.

ALICE: Parv—exactly how rich are you?

(This was the best part. This is when the crowd went really quiet. All eyes were on Parv.)

PARV: Ah my dear, Alice. A gentleman should never kiss and tell.

TIPSY: Pretend you're not a gentleman.

BIMSA: Can you kiss and tell past fifty million?

PARV: (smiling wryly) Does it matter? Aren't we here all having a good time? Sharing each other's company? And a good bottle of wine?

(By now I'm looking down at the table and scratching my scalp all over as if it were being bitten ferociously by head lice.)

ME: Rich people don't hang with poor people. Rich people don't like poor people. Poor people make rich people embarrassed. Rich people don't want to know the truth. Rich people turn their heads from poverty.

PARV: That's utter crap. Everyone turns their head from poverty. No one wants to see anyone suffering. We had many wonderful encounters in your coffee shop. Maybe I just liked your company. Maybe it was nice to be with someone who wanted to share moments with me because of me rather than because of my pocketbook. And for the record, you aren't suffering. I've seen places of hell on this earth where people are scrounging for potable water.

ME: And you're helping them.

PARV: In fact, I am helping them. Hopefully.

BIMSA: Where, for example?

PARV: For example, we have an animal sanctuary in Thailand.

(At this point I choke on my wine.)

PARV: Are you OK?

ME: Sorry. Just swallowed wrong.

(I shoot Bimsa a "Don't say anything!" look.)

PARV: The sanctuary operates under the guise of providing a home for suffering animals. But the donations we take in, largely from wealthy contributors, are actually used for a water project in India. Potable wells so women in rural farming areas do not have to walk miles for a bucket of water. So yes, ladies and gentlemen—gentleman—I have seen the seedy side of the world and even I—wealthy privileged, snobby, inconsiderate, dismissive rich bastard—can understand what's important in this world.

(We all squirm a moment and bashfully look about.)

PARV: Now, is there anything this rich asshole can get you?

BIMSA: (raising his hand) I would like a chocolate soufflé please.

(laughter)

ALICE: I would like the bananas flambé please. Bananas foster, that is.

TIPSY: Crème Bavaroise for me.

PARV: And you? What would make you stop hating me for a second?

ME: (chuckling slightly) I don't hate you. I just hate the other side of the world.

TIPSY: She means men.

BIMSA: She means straight men.

PARV: Zabaglione and fresh berries?

ME: Extra zabaglione

PARV: If that will make us friends again.

CRUSE TIPS:

Stay Clear of Passengers from Hell

Number One:
　　People are on a cruise for the same things: food, booze, sex.

Number Two:
　　People are not on a cruise to look at the ocean. Ironic. The water is annoying to them and they spend their days avoiding it. This explains why on "sea days" the passengers engage in any and all activities that divert their attention so they will not have to look at this splendid offering of nature. I mean, who would want to gaze at a vast, piercing-blue, awe-inspiring, body of water with whales and dolphins and seabirds and rolling white-foamed waves—when you could do line dancing instead? Sign me up. The Bead Jewelry Club from Schenectady might be fun as well. In short, I'd rather have a bad case of hemorrhoids.

ON SHIP:
The Weaponry of Ultimatums

I didn't like the way dinner ended. It was all too suspicious. I explained this to Tipsy and she fully agreed.

TIPSY: I still think he's got something up his sleeve. I don't trust men. I don't trust rich men. I don't trust rich, good-looking men. Although I wouldn't turn one down if one came my way. He does remind me so of Emile De Becque. Bastard.

ME: Yup. I need to take care of this and have *the* conversation.

TIPSY: Good idea, although it won't get you anywhere. Men never tell the truth. They never answer a direct question. They're going to tell you only what they want you to know anyway.

ME: Couldn't agree more. But I'm putting the question out there anyway. I'm so totally over this duplicitous behavior.

TIPSY: Sneaky, you mean.

ME: Sneaky, indeed. One minute in one city. Jetting off to another. Shows up here and then reveals some secret rich life. All that bullshit in Trieste. What the hell was he doing there?

I made arrangements to meet for late afternoon cocktails. Not that cocktails had to be in the late afternoon, but the idea of late afternoon sipping of champagne sounded so Deborah Kerr and Cary Grant. One needed only an old fashioned flat-topped glass filled with pink champagne.

Around five-thirty, I saw him waiting for me near the three-deck-high gold spiral. He found a table near the baby grand that seemed so appropriate for pink champagne and his Dolce & Gabbana jacket. I, on the other hand, showed up in black leggings, black sporty Nikes, and a black Michael Kors hoodie. I wanted to be in all black with no part of my body being displayed or adorned with a color other than black. This was purposeful as I remember he had given me some bullcrap line during one of our earlier encounters about how nice I looked in pastels. "That bird's egg blue is so perfect with your eyes and skin." I wonder how many times he had used that line. I probably could find it on page 1 of the "Men's Guide to the Most Nauseating Lines to be Used on Women."

PARV: I am delighted to see you, as always.
(Jeesh—the cornball lines right off the bat)
PARV: Would you like some champagne, or perhaps a martini?
ME: I would, indeed. In fact, I would love one of those delicious lychee martinis. If we stay here long enough, I might have two.
PARV: Well then, I hope we do stay here long enough.
ME: And while we're at it, see if you can procure some of those delicious canapes. I'm starving.
PARV: Certainly.

Parv signaled for the waiter—and negotiated for some tidbits from the bar tidbits menu. Eventually our drinks arrived—my lychee martini and his glass of Scotch. I'm not sure why men drink Scotch. I think it has something to do with their being James Bond-wannabees. If only Parv had that lovely Scottish accent. He might get something from me. He might have gotten it a long time ago. But thus far, the only thing he's gotten from me are looks of curiosity mixed with expressions of "you are so full of shit."

ME: (thinking this was a good lead-off line) I do so hate ships.
PARV: Pardon? Did you say you "hate" ships?

ME: I did say I hate ships. I think I might even despise them. I can't stand being trapped like a little animal in a limited amount of space. If I stay on this ship any longer, I will start to pace back and forth like a lion in a zoo. Or I might begin to rock my body back and forth over and over like a mad gorilla that's been encaged for forty years.

PARV: You think this lovely seventeen-deck, one-hundred-and-fifty-gross-tons vessel is a tiny cage?

ME: I do. I think it's full of too many people. I think the cabins aren't big enough to swing a cat in. I think the distance between my stateroom and a lifeboat is lightyears.

PARV: So, you are afraid of the water?

ME: I'm not afraid of the bloody water! I'm afraid of all the morons on board who don't even look at the water. I'm afraid of the simpletons who spend all their time at karaoke or filling their fat faces on crap food from the buffet covered in human snot and phlegm.

PARV: My my. Even after I put you in that lovely stateroom, you still feel this way?

ME: I do. And on that topic, *why* did you put me—us—me especially, in those "lovely staterooms."? I don't understand. What do you want from me? What's my bill for that stateroom?

PARV: Your "bill?" Your bill is nothing. Other than your company. Other than your friendship. Other than your continued presence in my life. Hopefully.

ME: Really? Because I think that's a load of crap!

(Parv registers a look of surprise.)

ME: I think anyone who wants me in his life wouldn't move around in the shadows—showing up every now and then—appearing out of nowhere like Dracula standing on the lawn under a moonlit sky.

PARV: Really you have quite the imagination. Hopefully I don't look like a vampire.

ME: But you come and go like one.

(The martinis have started to kick in.)

ME: Who are you? What are you? Why do you keep showing up?

PARV: Do you not want me to show up?

ME: I want you to be human and not some blood-sucking illusion.

PARV: It sounds as though you want to pick a fight.

ME: Damn right, I do! I want to pick a fight! I'm pissed about this whole weird thing that has been going on for what? Over a year? Curious encounters in my coffee shop? Just happen to be there? Just happen to be in town? Just happen to show up in Trieste? Just happen to work near my yoga studio? That all seems a bit suspicious.

PARV: Sometimes things do "just happen." Life is random. Not planned.

ME: I don't think life is random at all. I think everything that happens is laid out in some strange order. Like the throw of dice. After a while, patterns start to emerge.

PARV: Well then, I hope the throw of the dice will keep you in my life.

ME: For what purpose?

PARV: Does there have to be a purpose other than friendship?

ME: Ya. I think there does. I think there has to be continuity and objective.

PARV: My objective is to have you more involved in my life. My objective has been that from the start. My objective is not to scare you away with aggressive gestures and quick-to-the-draw advances. I would like to have a relationship. I would like to have a physical relationship. In fact, I am wondering why you have given me no signs of interest.

ME: A physical relationship? Like sex? Is that the word you're after?

PARV: Sex. Yes. Of course.

ME: Well that's interesting. Because from the moment I first saw you, I thought you were hot as hell. I think I caught myself drooling a couple of times. I'm a healthy woman. I would have liked some hot, wake up sore sex. That would have been great.

PARV: But you gave me no indication.

ME: But *you* gave *me* no indication.

PARV: Well if I didn't, then I was a fool. I most definitely would like to.

ME: This is really stupid. Because I think it would have been far hotter if you had just pulled me toward you at some point and kissed me so hard my brains would fall out.

PARV: I can do that, of course. But I am not a caveman.

ME: I think a caveman is OK every now and then. Sometimes you gotta just act and stop talking about it.

PARV: Then let's make a plan.

ME: What exactly is a *plan?* We will have sex and then what? I won't have any idea where you are and you will suddenly pop up like a jack-in-the box?

PARV: Why can't we just enjoy? Why must there be a *plan?* Why can't we just have a beautiful night? No strings. No drama.

ME: "No strings? No drama?"

PARV: Exactly. We just take things in stride and see where it leads.

ME: That sounds great. And just so we're on the same page, I interpret "no strings, no drama" as no commitment. No latching on. No ownership.

PARV: That would be a good definition.

ME: Perfect! Because that situation works both ways. No strings, no drama for me or you. We do what we need to do and then go our merry ways—and no one cares about what the other one does because there is no ownership. Just pleasure.

PARV: For the moment, I think that's the ideal way to work into a relationship.

ME: Okay. I'm think that's a great plan. No strings and no drama.

PARV: So, shall we put it to the test after we finish our drinks? Perhaps a nice dinner by candlelight? Some wine? Dancing on the balcony? I would like to give you what I imagine every woman in the world would desire.

ME: Wow. Tempting. But here's some feedback. Do you really think that's what every woman desires? Let me clue you in. Every woman desires to be treated with dignity. Every woman desires to get paid the same as the asshole men she has to work next to every day, who spend their time treating her like a dog, and then walk away at the end of the week with far more for doing far less. Every woman desires to have someone cherish her but not objectify her. For now, I'm going to take a last sip of my delicious lychee martini and then I'm going for a walk. "No strings. No drama."? I'll have to give that one a think.

TIPSY: So, now what?

ME: Now I get off this fucking ship at the first fishing village, and Emile can stick his "no strings, no drama" up his well-groomed rich ass.

BIMSA: I'd like to see that ass.

CRUISE TIPS:
Find a Place of Tranquility

Number One:

There is no such thing. Cruise ships are a constant exercise in audio torture. Your sanity will be tested each time the Cruise Director makes his super-exciting-fun-events-of-the-day announcement. Each time you will imagine your hands around his throat.

Number Two:

Don't think for a second hiding in your cabin will help. The announcements can and will reach that sacred inner chamber. Note: the announcement will reach inside the cabin only if the captain has some extremely important message. This should make you feel better already. An announcement so vital, that it forces the captain to give you bad news directly in your cabin, should surely be a sign of comfort. There are usually only two reasons the captain's voice would invade the privacy of your cabin: nausea-inducing bad weather or the ship is entering a zone of infectious insects. More Scotch needed.

ON SHIP:

What Officer Tipsy Reported

During the several days we've been onboard, Officer Tipsy has provided a continuous stream of live reporting. Alice is convinced Tipsy secretly works for a major television network.

BIMSA: Ha! You're vexed only because she caught you and that Australian wanker kissing at midnight during the jumbo screen showing of Hugh Jackman.

ALICE: Hugh Jackman is not the name of a movie, Uncle.

BIMSA: Lassie, I hardly care what the name of the movie is when Hugh Jackman is on the screen. And forty feet of him makes it so worth whatever the movie is.

TIPSY: I don't like that Australian boy. He's a bit too smooth-acting for me.

ME: Smooth? Does that mean over-the-top obsequious?

TIPSY: It does, indeed.

ALICE: I like him. And he's a great kisser.

BIMSA: Eeewwww. Stop. I don't want to think of any boy touching my niece.

ALICE: I'm seventeen.

BIMSA: And you should be locked up in a nunnery with the key thrown away.

TIPSY: Bimsa, will you please shut up! I have something more interesting to report on than mini-dick Australian boys.

BIMSA: Go on then, missus.

TIPSY: After I saw Alice with boomerang boy, I walked around the corner to fetch a soft serve twist from that handsome Macedonian lad.

BIMSA: Now that's a funny concept.

TIPSY: Don't knock it 'til you've tried it. Macedonians like large plates of meat. Need I say more?

ME: Tipsy, what the hell? Skip the Macedonian and move on. What did you stumble across this time?

TIPSY: I stumbled across our friend Parv. At midnight. With a tall glass of bubbly in one hand.

ME: So far that doesn't seem to be a crime. In fact, I should have a tall glass of bubbly in one hand while watching jumbo images of Eric Bana.

BIMSA: Hugh Jackman and his magic wand.

ME: I like Eric Bana.

TIPSY: But it was what he had in the other hand that fascinated me.

BIMSA: His willy? Was he wanking off in the moonlight?

TIPSY: In his other hand was a long-legged, big-breasted, dark-haired girl, I'd say about the age of Alice.

(All chatter suddenly ceased.)

ME: Doing what, exactly?

TIPSY: Ah. I thought you'd be interested. Doing nothing. Just holding her hand.

ME: Holding her hand like "You're my sweet niece," or holding her hand like "I can't wait to put my magic wand up your backside."?

TIPSY: I don't think she was his niece.

ME: Fuck me. Fuck me blind.

BIMSA: You said it, girl! Amen. The cry of the brotherhood!

ME: Did he see you?

TIPSY: Absolutely not! When I spy, I spy with complete discretion.

ALICE: Maybe he's trafficking?

BIMSA: That's it. You're off this ship at first port! Unless it's Wales.

ALICE: But Unc—first port is the Shetlands.

BIMSA: Perfect. Lots of sheep. Completely surrounded by water. You will never escape!

ALICE: It sounds like a scene from The Count of Monte Cristo.

TIPSY: Well, my dear. Whatever is or was Mr. Parv's motive for all this pomp and circumstance onboard, I just think there might be some nefarious activity going on you should know about.

ME: Thank you, Tipsy. You're a good friend.

BIMSA: I think he deserves death. Tipsy—run him over with your Elmco!

ME: Oh Bimsa, it might have been totally innocent.

BIMSA: Seriously, girl?

ME: Ok—I was just trying to remain open minded. But Tipsy is right. Why all the suites and wining and dining?

BIMSA: Face it, girl. You might have become part of his stable.

ME: I knew this cruise shit was a mistake. Crap. Crap. Crap.

TIPSY: Well, never mind. Just enjoy the fun. Come along. It's almost time for afternoon tea. I am especially fond of those nifty little chicken and cucumber sandwiches. And a nice hot pot of tea.

ALICE: I want scones and jam.

BIMSA: Maybe we'll run into Zorro. And you can give him a piece of your mind! That's all, though. Nothing from any part of your body lower than your mind.

ME: My mind right now is the lowest part of my body. Fucking hell.

CRUISE TIPS:

Be on Alert for Pot-Bellied Men Wearing Matching Grotesquely Bright Yellow Shirts and Gripping Crushed Beer Cans

Hell is thinking you've found the one place on the ship were no one will go and suddenly the Local Chapter of Veterans, Artillery Group arrives, comprised of 23 fat, old duffers who can't hear, and so they shout at each other for two hours, reminiscing about the war and complaining they can't get any of their military benefits, comparing who's got the biggest belly, who's got the longest military record, and who's got the oldest military record including, but not limited to, serving with Teddy Roosevelt's Rough Riders.

ON SHORE:
Pulling into Port

W e are now in port after three weeks of a tranquil transat-
lantic crossing. From hell.

Never mind the freezing cold, hostile, satanic body of water
continuously chomping at our asses. The rolls of water had crashed
against Deck 6, the size of which, performing some quick math,
equated to "pretty damn high."

By my estimate, the waves were somewhere near the size of a
small skyscraper. It was like a bad accident. I couldn't look away.
Mounds of icy water had threatened to break through the floor-to-
ceiling windows near which I sat sipping my porn star martini.

What would I have done if there were a life-threatening situation? An emergency? I weighed my options. Would I have donned
my bright orange, designer lifejacket, complete with a manual in-
flation tube and a whistle for attracting attention? Would I have
jumped in and possibly drowned in the titanic waters, in a brave
attempt to save others? Or would I have demonstrated calm to
other passengers by remaining in my warm alcove, snuggled up to
a friendly glass of alcohol? I chose the latter.

Most of the time, when the weather was rough, I stumbled
around like a drunk. Or was I drunk? After a while, the two con-
ditions went hand in hand.

CRUISE TIPS:
Bring *War and Peace* to Debarkation

If you think it's hard to get on the ship, try to get off. Just sayin'.

ON SHORE:

A Peerie Place

I'm used to large airports. I'm used to being bumped around and knocked over and plowed through by throngs of people all racing to and from their flights. Every man for himself and herself at large airports.

I'm used to waiting hours for my luggage and elbowing my way through the crowds to get a good position by the carousel.

In the Peerie Place, there are, by my estimate, no more than twenty people at any given time inside the airport terminal. The luggage carousel holds approximately five bags. There is one check-in counter and I'm fairly certain I saw my check-in agent also dragging a refueling hose across the tarmac.

When I got off the small, twenty-four-seat jet, I had but fifty feet to walk before landing inside the terminal. I'd purposely not checked luggage to avoid the hassle of a long wait to retrieve it. Little did I know.

My pre-ordered taxi driver was inside the terminal. By the luggage carousel. Standing with a name card. My name. She was easy to spot. She was the only one in the terminal other than myself and the hose-dragging-refueling-combo check-in agent.

Mags was her name. Short for Magnuson, she told me. We walked another fifty feet to her Vauxhall station wagon. I, of course, tried to get in the driver's side. I wish these countries would put the bloody steering wheel on the correct side of the car.

I got in the front seat with Mags as I thought it would be rather rude to sit in the back. This was a big mistake. Not because of Mags; she was an angel. It was because she had a bit of a lead foot and the terrain we were crossing was a compilation of curves and steep cliffs. Both, if navigated incorrectly, would land Mags and me directly into the cold North Sea. I could have withstood the steep curves and high precipices had it not been for the trees.

Actually, had it been for the trees. Because there were no trees. An entire country without trees. It was like looking at miles of snow. After a while, your eyes can't distinguish horizon from sky.

And so, my stomach was a stone's throw from puking all over Mags' nice Vauxhall.

Whereas there were no trees, there were miles of unbelievable shots of crashing blue ocean against high cliffs. I saw no less than a million sheep. Followed by strange little horses that were a trademark of these islands.

Mags gave me the whole rundown. The islands had been a gift from Norway. Ah, I thought. *That explains why everyone looks Scandinavian yet speaks with a Scottish accent.* Try to imagine a Viking with his metal horns and shield of arms walking around speaking like Shrek. It's rather funny.

Why am I here? Oh yes. I'm here because I have a mission in Edinburgh. That mission is to go back to the scene of a crime. And to get back to the scene of the crime, one has to carefully retrace one's steps.

My steps, unfortunately, involved a trip to the Peerie Place. The little islands. The Shetlands. Caught somewhere between Norway to the east and Iceland to the west. Don't go to the Shetlands if you want to stay warm. Don't go to the Shetlands if you want to cut down a Christmas tree. Don't go to the Shetlands if you don't like wind or sheep or people with accents so strong you have no bloody clue what they are saying.

Mags drove me to my hotel, which was on the edge of the

main city. City? Not so much. Not big enough to swing a cat in. I could walk the entire town, end to end, in a matter of fifteen large "Captain, may I?" steps. Nevertheless, Mags insisted on giving me a map of the town so I wouldn't get lost. How could I get lost? There are exactly six buildings, one harbor, five lampposts, and one trash can painted with Viking designs.

I made a beeline for one of the six buildings that was the post office. After circling through the two aisles multiple times, I was finally asked what I was looking for.

ME: I'm looking for postcards.

SCOTTISH NORWEGIAN VIKING PERSON: But there are no postcards in a post office.

ME: No? Ok. That makes sense. Why would I find anything to mail in a place to mail it? So, where would I find postcards?

PERSON: In the card shop, of course.

ME: Of course. Ok. Last question. I can buy stamps here—correct?

PERSON. Spot on.

After posting my postcards in the post office, I grabbed a local flyer about native birds. The Peerie Place is known for birds, especially puffins. In fact, most of the shops sell "Puffin Poo", which is essentially chocolate and God knows what other ingredient, but I guess it could be shit.

To illustrate my point about the smallness of this town, I need only cite the incident with the local flyer about native birds. I was walking along, and I heard a constant honking. After two blocks, I realized the driver was honking at me. And after a minute, I realized the reason that person was honking at me is because, two blocks back, I had dropped my flyer about native birds. This good citizen of the Peerie Place was honking to let me know I had dropped my flyer. This doesn't happen in New York. If someone were honking at me after two blocks in New York, I would stop cold, walk up to the car, and beat the shit out of the driver. And I would use my best New Jersey accent while doing so.

So the taxi driver, in Edinburgh, warned me the first time about going here. He said it was cold and bleak. I guess he had never been to Iowa.

The second time, I did not get a warning from my taxi driver in Edinburgh. But I did get warned by my taxi driver in the Peerie Place, Mags, that this place would grow on me.

Sure. I could see that. A bit like the Gulag with a Scottish twist.

Unfortunately, it seems Mags might have been on to something. That night, I had cold North Sea fresh halibut and roasted potatoes. I had prosecco and warm rhubarb pudding. I took a photo of the waves crashing about and caught a white spray from the rotating beam off the lighthouse. And right before snuggling down into my soft white sheets and right before pulling the warm down comforter over my ears, I realized the Peerie Place was the last jaunt I made before I had seen my 18-minute man on the prior visit. So I shut my eyes and decided this was a place of luck. I would go back to Edinburgh and march right back to that coffee shop and the 18-minute man would be there. And he would be just as I remembered him. Only one minor problem. I have no recollection of what he looked like.

The next morning, Mags fetched me once again for the twenty-mile drive to the airport. We stopped short of the airport as the signal arms came down at the railroad crossing. It took my mind a minute to kick in because there is no railroad here. It's too small.

MAGS: No trains here. We're sitting on the runway.
ME: On a live runway?
MAGS: Yup. See that FlyBe about to land? That's your plane.
ME: Just sheep and Shetland ponies and puffins.
MAGS: That's about it.
ME: No trees.

MAGS: No trees. A lot of wind.

ME: Who wouldn't want to live here? That's what I say.

MAGS: It grows on you.

ME: I've been meaning to ask. What does "peerie" mean?

MAGS: Little.

ON SHORE:
Christmas Dinner at Bimsa's

A s many times as I have been to the UK, there are still cultural nuances that elude me. Part of this has to do with how I grew up, of course, and how things work in other parts of the world. And part of this has to do with Bimsa's family being completely crackers. Maybe that's why they pull apart the Christmas crackers?

Imagine you are sitting in a British comedy theatre and watching this endless strange cast of characters in motion. Or at least that's what I did. I picked a prime spot, in front of the fireplace, plopping my bottom on a flowery cushioned chair, settled down with a glass of prosecco, and watched the endless parade of nut cases coming in and out of the picture.

BIMSA: So, what notes have you taken, you rude little minx?

ME: Can I start with your cousin Valerie?

BIMSA: Perfect! Bloody crazy bitch!

ME: It's just that she knows everything. Everything. No matter what subject you bring up, she's the expert. Goes on and on and on. I just about smacked her a few minutes ago.

BIMSA: Oh, how I wish you had. Great fun! Did she tell you what a wine connoisseur she is?

ME: Boy did she! Once again, she knew it all. And she has a membership to some boring restaurant if I ever want to go with her, which would be a cold day in hell. And she has some brother who makes a million Euros a day, and yet she works in some department store. What am I missing?

BIMSA: She loves that million-Euros-a-day story. He probably owes someone a million Euro a day. Lives in Greece somewhere, God knows what he does, and somehow manages to have a lot of money. I think he runs weapons. Or worse, is a gigolo to rich Greek women. He's rather a perv.

ME: Zorba

BIMSA: Zorba the Freak.

ME: Reminder—we have Edinburgh in a few days. You go do whatever you have to do. I have a mission.

BIMSA: Ah,, yes. Not just any mission. *The* mission! The quest to find the 18-minute man.

ME: You really have to stop calling him the "18-minute man." It sounds so wrong.

BIMSA: Well I hope you find him and he has more stamina than a mere 18 minutes!

ME: Because you're such a rock star?

BIMSA: I have endurance, stamina, and the will to hang on even in the roughest of storms.

MF: Define "roughest of storms."

BIMSA: Funky breath.

ME: Ah. That would make one shut down fairly fast. Hang on. Why are you at a disadvantage. In my world, the guy has to face me. In your world, the guy is facing the back of your head. How do you smell anyone's breath?

BIMSA: Oh, child. You are so unenlightened.

ME: Who is that woman over there? The one with the world's longest cigarette?

BIMSA: That's my auntie Colleen. She never lights it. She just carries it around because she is crazy and still thinks she's living in the time of F. Scott.

ME: And what about that one over there? The one in the jodh-purs and riding boots?

BIMSA: The only thing missing is a small riding crop for her to beat something or someone. That's my other aunt, Aunt Kim. Total nutcase. Rich as hell. Does nothing all day but hang with the Who's Who at the riding club or the gun club.

ME: She shoots?

BIMSA: No. She has a bird dog. She takes him to the gun club for practice on retrieving big old dead birds.

ME: Don't look now, but your Cousin Valerie just plunked her rather large caboose on the sofa between your nephews.

BIMSA: She probably thinks she has a shot.

ME: I'm sure she does. Never mind that she's at least thirty years older than those boys. Never mind that they're family. A bit pervy.

BIMSA: Watch when she gets drunk. That's fairly entertaining. She'll start to dance and move her massive butt across the room. I would pay someone to smack her across the face a few times. With a large dick.

ME: You are seriously disturbed.

BIMSA: I'm Scottish. We don't mince words.

ME: Speaking of mince, I believe I've popped no fewer than twenty of those little mince meat pies down my throat. If I eat one more of these sausage rolls, I'm going to barf. They are like popcorn. I can't stop shoving them in my mouth.

BIMSA: Right?

ME: Bimsa, please tell me we are not going to eat a big meal after all these starters?

BIMSA: Seriously, girl? We have turkey, sausages, stuffing, Brussels sprouts, parsnips, broccoli, carrots, garlic bread, roasted potatoes, meat gravy, bread gravy, and that's all I can remember at present because I'm seriously drunk.

ME: I guess that means we will be having a light dessert?

BIMSA: No, lass—it means we will be having a dessert that you light. Flaming fucking Christmas pudding! And that's one of probably five. And about four hours after we eat, they will bring it all out again so we can indulge in the leftovers.

ME: I'm in hell. Does this mean I have to stay another four hours?

BIMSA: Oh God yes. We still have games. My favorite is the running from room to room with a potato held between your thighs.

ME: What the hell are you talking about?

BIMSA: And you have to "poop" the potato into a bucket.

ME: Sweet Jesus. What deviant thought up that game?

BIMSA: That would be my Uncle Andy. He will make sure you have to toss back a shot if you drop the potato.

ME: Your family is going to kill me. Please don't let them kill me. I have to get to Edinburgh. See if my secret guy is still there.

BIMSA: He'd be a fucking skeleton if his stupid ass is still sitting there!

ON SHORE:
Our Missions

Bimsa's mission was clear. He was hell-bent on dragging me around to all points in the UK for the purpose of meeting his family, but more likely, for Bimsa to demonstrate to his family he has at least one friend in the world who isn't stark raving mad. This was ironic. As it turns out. most of Bimsa's family were stark raving mad. Or at least demonstrated aspects of being stark raving mad.

Although I had teased Bimsa about the need to show me off, I knew he needed some family time. He had been abroad for a number of years and the trips home were not as frequent as he'd hoped.

And although I'm Bimsa's best female friend, his best friend for life was his brother. Bimsa needed an emotional purge with his brother and once the two of them got together, they would spend most of the time in a nearby pub, dissecting their worlds and running diagnostics on the current state of their lives. This would all be done with a lot of Scotch and unhealthy food, which is the best type of food if one is going to drink.

My mission was clear. I had been to Edinburgh several months before. I started something and I needed to finish it. So Edinburgh was on the list of our visitations. Bimsa's brother lived there.

ON SHORE:
Revisiting the Scene of the Crime

I walked the hill to the coffee shop. Tracing my path. Taking the exact same route. Stopping the exact same places. Wondering if it was possible for life to have people's paths cross twice or if a serendipitous event happens only once and if you don't grab it then and there, you will never have another opportunity.

What if that man were the better half of me? What if I were his soulmate? And did he, for one split second, think the same? Did he wonder if he should have offered more than just a simple-ass gesture of "You're welcome to stay in Edinburgh as long as you wish."?

And so I walked up the hill, toward the bronze statue of the Scottish soldier with the tall hat and handlebar mustache, astride a great steed and readied for battle.

How stupid is this? Fucking stupid. What the fuck? This is totally fucked. Have I lost my fucking mind?

And no matter what I did, I could concentrate on the mission at hand. I kept getting lost in thought about odd things on the street. The all-you-can-eat dim sum restaurant so appropriately named Saigon Saigon. I was tempted to knock on the door and point out to the proprietor that the food item and the city had little in common other than they both had some affiliation and history with Asia. Maybe it was a ruse. Maybe the promise of all-you-can-eat dim sum lured the unsuspecting tourist flies into the trap of endless dim sum and then out from behind the walls jumped someone in a Ho Chi Minh mask.

And why is there nowhere in the world where one can escape McDonald's? Is nothing sacred anymore?

Back to the coffee shop. Another slight problem was looming. I couldn't actually remember what this guy looked like. I saw him for all of twenty minutes. I spoke to him for all of thirty seconds. I couldn't honestly remember one detail of his face or hair or eyes. I couldn't remember if he was short or tall. I think he was fit. I think he was slightly greying. But then I could be confusing this guy with a character I had been watching on a detective series.

And then I got distracted by the massive tower in the middle of the city. I knew what the massive tower was, in fact. Because the first time I had been to Edinburgh, I was drawn to the tower. Not a tower so much as a spiky monument. So I plowed my way through the throngs on the sidewalk and then wiggled through the crowds on the opposite side of the street to ascertain why the Scots would build a monument of this magnitude in the middle of the city.

When I finally made it to the other side, I looked up at a statue looming from the top with an inscription beneath.

Shit! Am I stupid! I've read every one of this man's books and had no fucking clue he was Scottish. No wonder people think Americans are total tossers.

Did my guy have a mustache? Did he have glasses? Maybe he was gay? Maybe the guy he'd been ensconced in deep conversation with was his partner?

Bimsa had volunteered to come along. But I was worried Bimsa's gaydar would suddenly go off and he would burst my bubble by revealing my fantasy man was gay.

I chickened out. I decided to go into Saigon Saigon and taste the Vietnamese dim sum. But it was really pissing me off. *It* being me. I was really pissing myself off about this stupid 18-minute man.

ON SHORE:
The 18-Minute Day of Reckoning

I'm motivated by fear. And the biggest thing I fear is not doing something. It pisses me off. It pisses me off when I don't do the thing I wanted to do because I was too chicken to try.

I spent an entire year mentally kicking myself because I didn't swim out to the floating dock at Moose Lake. It was a beautiful and oddly warm August day. In other parts of the world, August might be known as a hot month, but at Moose Lake, August touches the edge of autumn. Oddly warm because Moose Lake is high up in the northern latitudes near the Continental Divide, where the rivers turn north toward the Hudson Bay.

Polar bears are known to wear earmuffs and Norwegian Dale sweaters, even in the heart of summer. But that day, it was warm enough to venture a swim in the old glacier lake. It was warm enough to swim the not-so-many yards out to the floating dock as I would have when I was a fearless young girl.

If I don't do what I want to do, then I sit around and dwell on what I might have missed. Ironically, if I do the thing I want to do, and it turns out to be a flaccid experience, then I will sit around and lament and moan for other reasons, but I will have at least tested myself. At worst, I might chastise myself for believing reality could match or even vaguely resemble my imagination. It's the proverbial vicious cycle.

BIMSA: Fearless young girl? Is that the same as dumbass young girl?

ME: At least I had a life once upon a time. Now I get a bad case of hemorrhoids just from worrying about an outcome.

BIMSA: I get a bad case of hemorrhoids at least once a month from forgetting to worry about the outcome.

ME: So, who's the dumbass?

BIMSA: The real question is, who's the sore ass?

(Bimsa's sense of humor continues to elude me.)

BIMSA: So, today is the big day.

ME: Today is the big day.

BIMSA: What are you really going to do today?

ME: I don't know.

BIMSA: Why does that not surprise me?

ME: I think I will start walking. And see where my feet carry me.

BIMSA: Now there's a plan. A wee loosely woven, but a plan. Ok girl, so get your ass out the door! Off with you!

ME: Ok. Coat's on. Last-minute check for any odd bits on my face.

(Bimsa looks me up and down and side to side.)

BIMSA: No odd bits. Not a hair growing out of place. Show me the teeth.

(I show him a big toothy display.)

BIMSA: No black bits. No seeds. No green strings. Nothing hanging from the nose. Now go, girl. You're ready.

ME: I'm off. I'm walking through the door and straight up that hill. And when I land inside that coffee shop, something will be waiting.

BIMSA: Hopefully a man. Unless you're suddenly crossing over into the better side of life?

ME: No, Bimsa. I'm still that boring straight woman, I'm afraid.

BIMSA: No worries. There's plenty of boring straight men out there. Unfortunately. Hugh Jackman. Omar Sy. So, get that your straight ass of yours out there.

And after demonstratively tossing my brown and red wool scarf around my neck, fluffing up my hair, and sweeping my black quilted coat over shoulders, I place one final dab of eucalyptus moisturizer on my lips, take a deep breath, and begin the climb.

The blocks pass by. My legs are moving down sidewalks and up steps and across parks without instruction. I expect reality will meet me at the top. I know imagination is pushing me on.

About the Author

Bert Bartz's books are a humorous and acerbic portrayal of friendships, romance, and annoying life circumstances. Her most recent works are *You Are Now Entering, Conquering the Crow,* and *The Fail Mary Plan.* She hopes you will find and enjoy all her books. To contact Bert, you can reach her at BertBartz.Books@gmail.com.

Printed in the United States
By Bookmasters